Adventures
at Pebble Pond

Webster's Journey

By Joy Ann Daffern

Dear Charlotte & Olivia,
Thank you for
joining the adventure.
Best, Joy

ISBN: 1499390726
ISBN 13: 9781499390728
Library of Congress Control Number: 2014908768
CreateSpace Independent Publishing Platform
North Charleston, South Carolina

To my little ducklings,
Dinky, Bubba & Sweat Pea.

I love you all oh so very much.

Webster is a duck. He looks like any ordinary duck. He has a bill for a mouth, two webbed feet, and feathers that are fluffy like a cloud. Although Webster may look like any other duck, he sure doesn't act like one.

Webster, you see, is not a very good swimmer. All his brothers and sisters can't wait to get into the water to play, but not Webster.

One day Webster stays behind when his brothers and sisters leave to play in the pond. Webster's brothers and sisters tease him.

"What kind of a duck can't swim well?" they ask. What kind of duck indeed?

Webster thinks and thinks. Since he always looks on the bright side of things, he gets the idea that this could only mean one thing: He is not a duck.

"Mommy, I don't think I'm a duck," Webster says.

"What makes you think you're not a duck?" his mother asks.

"I don't swim very well and all ducks can swim well so that means I'm not a duck," Webster tells her.

"Just because you are not a strong swimmer yet doesn't mean you're not a duck. You have other special gifts," Webster's mother tells him.

Webster looks down at himself not understanding what his mother means. He has no special gifts. He only has a bill for a mouth, two webbed feet, and feathers. No, he must not be a duck, but what could he be?

"If I'm not a duck, I must be something else," Webster says happily. He decides he must go out into the world to find out what he really is.

"Mommy, I am going on an adventure to find out who I am. It will be a long and hard trip so can you please pack me a snack?" Webster asks her.

Webster's mother smiles warmly at her youngest duckling when he tells her of his plans.

"How about I pack you your favorite foods— plants, grasses, and earthworms?" Webster's mother tells him.

"Yum, yum!" Webster happily tells his mother.

With his backpack of goodies slung over his shoulder, Webster puts one webbed foot in front of the other and heads out into the great big world.

After walking what feels like hundreds and hundreds of miles, Webster comes face-to-face with his friend Stenchy the Skunk. Webster likes Stenchy, even though Stenchy is a skunk, and Stenchy likes Webster, even though Webster isn't a skunk.

"Hi, Webster!" Stenchy says excitedly. "What are you up to?"

Exhausted, Webster plunks down his backpack. "I've just walked a hundred miles from home, and I'm very tired," he says. Stenchy looks confused for a moment because he can still see Webster's home, but everyone knows skunks don't see well so that must explain it.

"Where are you heading?" Stenchy asks.

"I'm on an adventure to find out who I really am," Webster says. "Maybe I'm a skunk like you!"

Now Stenchy is really confused because Webster does not look like a skunk, but the idea that his friend might be like him interests him.

"Can you give off a smell like rotten eggs?"
Stenchy asks proudly.

"Aaaah, definitely not," Webster says.

"Can you squeal, screech, or grunt?" Stenchy asks. Webster tries, but a quack comes out instead.

"No, but I can quack," Webster says.

"Oh, like a duck," says Stenchy. Like a duck indeed.

Webster smiles and says, "Well, we may not both be skunks, but we'll always be friends." Stenchy smiles back and wishes Webster luck on his journey.

After walking what *seems* to be a few hundred more miles, Webster sees his friend Scooter the Squirrel. By now, Webster is very hungry and tired. Scooter asks where Webster is going with his backpack.

As Webster begins to eat his yummy plants, grass and earthworms, he explains that he is off on an adventure to find his true self. Scooter is confused.

"Where did you lose yourself?" Scooter asks. "I can help you look." Webster laughs and quacks so hard, he thinks he might lose his feathers. Webster explains that he feels he may not be a duck, although he now knows he's definitely not a skunk. Scooter excitedly suggests that maybe Webster is a squirrel.

"Would you like to live up in a tree?" Scooter asks.

Webster looks at his webbed feet and says, "I don't think I can."

"Do you like nuts?" Scooter questions.

"No, I'm allergic to nuts, but I do like to eat plants, grass, and earthworms."

"Oh, like a duck," replies Scooter. Like a duck indeed.

"We may not both be squirrels, but we'll always be friends," Webster says. Scooter smiles back and wishes Webster luck on his journey.

The sun is starting to set when Webster decides to stop and rest after what must be several hundred more miles. It is getting dark, and Webster is starting to worry when he hears a familiar sound.

"Ri--bitt. Ri--bitt."

Webster hurries around the bend and comes
face-to-face with his friend Croaker the Frog.

"Croaker!" cries Webster. "I'm so happy to see a friend. I've been walking for thousands of miles, and I'm getting very tired."

Croaker looks amused because he knows Webster lives just on the other side of the pond.

"Well, why have you walked so far?" Croaker asks.

"To find out who I really am, although I know now that I'm not a skunk or a squirrel— maybe I'm a frog!" Webster proudly declares.

Croaker, wanting to help, asks, "Well, do you have a long, sticky tongue?"

Webster gulps. "That would be a big N-O."

"Are you able to jump really high?"

Webster dances around on his webbed feet,
which stay firmly on the ground.

"No, but I can waddle."

"Oh, like a duck," Croaker says. Like a duck
indeed.

As Webster picks up his backpack, he turns to Croaker and smiles. "Well, we may not both be frogs, but we'll always be friends." Croaker smiles back and wishes Webster luck on his journey.

It is now getting dark and cold. Webster is tired and sad. How he wishes he were home, but home is such a long ways away. It will take him forever to get home with his little webbed feet. If he could swim, he would jump in the water and be home in no time.

Webster then remembers his mother telling him he has many special gifts. What special gifts? All he has is his bill for a mouth, two webbed feet, and feathers.

He has feathers! Webster realizes he may not be able to swim well, but maybe he can fly!

Webster begins to flap his feathers, and before he can quack, he is soaring through the air.

"I can fly! I can fly!" cries Webster as he flies toward home. He not only can fly, but he also can fly fast! Wow, what an amazing flier he is.

In no time at all, he finds himself standing in front of his home, with his mother waiting right outside the door with the porch light on. He snuggles up to his mother.

"I'm a duck!" Webster announces.

Webster's mother smiles at her little duckling and says, "What a special duck indeed."

Joy Ann Daffern is an entertainment executive residing in Los Angeles. She holds a master's degree in business administration, and although she loves her job, she has always longed to write children's books.

Daffern grew up in San Francisco and never had an opportunity to learn to swim. She's married with three children, and everyone in the family (including the bulldog) swims better than she does. Being the aquatic outsider inspired her to write *Adventures at Pebble Pond: Webster's Journey.*